THE PRINCE
AND THE PAUPER

STEP INTO CLASSICS™

THE PRINCE
AND THE PAUPER

By Mark Twain

Adapted by Jane E. Gerver

Step into Classics™

Random House 🏠 New York

Copyright © 1999 by Random House, Inc.
Cover illustration copyright © 1999 by Brian Kotzky.
All rights reserved under International and Pan-American
Copyright Conventions. Published in the United States by
Random House, Inc., New York, and simultaneously in Canada by
Random House of Canada Limited, Toronto.

www.randomhouse.com/kids

Library of Congress Cataloging-in-Publication Data
Gerver, Jane E.
The prince and the pauper / by Mark Twain ; adapted by
Jane E. Gerver.   p.   cm.   (Step into classics)   SUMMARY: When young
Edward VI of England and a poor boy who resembles him exchange
places, each learns something about the other's very different station
in life.
ISBN 0-679-89213-3 (pbk.)
1. Edward VI, King of England, 1537–1553—Juvenile fiction.
[1. Edward VI, King of England, 1537–1553—Fiction.
2. Mistaken identity—Fiction.   3. Adventure and adventurers—Fiction.
4. England—Fiction.]   I. Twain, Mark, 1835–1910. Prince and the
pauper.   II. Title.   III. Series.
PZ7.G3264Pr   1999   [Fic]—dc21   98-41049

Printed in the United States of America 10 9 8 7 6 5 4 3 2 1
RANDOM HOUSE and colophon are registered trademarks
of Random House, Inc.
STEP INTO CLASSICS and colophon are trademarks
of Random House, Inc.

To Joseph and Michael

—J.E.G.

Contents

THE PRINCE
AND THE PAUPER

Chapter One

The Birth of the Prince and the Pauper

One day many years ago, in the city of London, two baby boys were born. One was Edward Tudor, the Prince of Wales. He was the king of England's son. The other baby, Tom, was born to a poor family named Canty.

"Hurrah!" The whole country celebrated Prince Edward's birth in grand style. People feasted and sang and danced for days. They could not stop talking about the rich baby wrapped in silks and satins in the palace.

But no one celebrated Tom Canty's birth, not even his own family. No one honored the new baby pauper wrapped in rags.

Tom Canty grew up in a rickety old house in Offal Court, in an alley near Pudding Lane in London. He shared a cramped room with his parents, grandmother, and twin sisters, Bet and Nan.

Fights broke out constantly in the alley. There was little to eat. And Tom's father forced his three children to beg in the streets for money.

Luckily for Tom, a kindly priest named Father Andrew lived in the same house. He taught Tom how to read and write English, and even a little Latin.

Father Andrew also told Tom stories about kings and queens, princes and princesses. The boy liked these lessons best of all.

How Tom longed to see a real prince! He read books about princes. He dreamed about princes. Soon he even began to *act* like a prince, with courtly speech and manners.

At first, his friends teased him. But by and by, they gained respect for Tom. He seemed to know so much. He could do and say such marvelous things. And he was good at helping people with their problems.

"Tom is such a wise boy!" everyone agreed.

But each day, after pretending to hold court as a prince, Tom had to go in the streets and beg for money. Then he would hurry home and try to sleep.

Because in his dreams, he was always a prince.

Chapter Two
Tom Meets the Prince

One January day, Tom took a long walk through London. He wandered around narrow lanes and wide streets until he had left the main city behind.

Down a quiet, lovely road, he came upon a grand and beautiful building. This was Westminster Palace, where the royal family lived.

In front of the palace was a set of golden gates. Stately guards, as still as statues, stood on each side. Countryfolk and people from the city watched from a distance. They hoped to see a glimpse of royalty.

Tom stood at the gates and peered up in awe at the lofty stone turrets on the palace. He moved aside as splendid carriages rolled up. The guards swung open the gates to let the carriages in.

Then Tom looked through the golden gates to the palace grounds. There stood a handsome, sturdy boy.

He was dressed in silks and satins. A little sword and dagger were at his hip. The sword and dagger were decorated with jewels. A large feather and a shining jewel adorned the boy's hat.

This boy was a real, live prince! Tom's heart leapt with joy. How could he get a closer look at the boy? Tom pushed against the bars of the gate.

At once a soldier grabbed Tom and sent him reeling. "Mind your manners, young beggar!" the soldier said. The people in the street jeered at Tom.

Inside the palace grounds, the young prince had seen what had happened. He sprang forward. His eyes flashed with anger.

"How dare you treat a poor lad like that!" the prince scolded the soldier. "Open the gates and let him in!"

The crowd cheered. "Long live the Prince of Wales!" they cried.

The soldiers opened the gates, and Tom passed through. Prince Edward Tudor came over to him.

"You look tired and hungry," he said kindly to Tom. "Come with me."

Edward took Tom into the palace. The

floors were highly polished, and the walls were hung with portraits and tapestries. Tom gawked at the wonderful sights.

At last, they reached a fancy set of rooms. The prince commanded a servant to bring them a meal. And what a meal it was! Tom had never seen or eaten such wonderful food. While Tom feasted, the prince asked him many questions.

"What is your name, lad?"

"Tom Canty, sir," Tom said shyly.

"What an odd name!" said the prince. "Where do you live?"

"Offal Court. Near Pudding Lane, sir."

"And do you have parents?"

"Yes, sir. And a grandmother and twin sisters also," Tom said.

"And how do they treat you?"

"My father and grandmother are cruel at times," Tom confessed. "But my mother is good to me—and so are my sisters, Nan and Bet."

"I have two sisters also," said the prince. "I am close to one sister, the lady Elizabeth. I am also fond of my cousin Lady Jane Grey. But my gloomy sister, the lady Mary—" He paused. "Tell me, Tom, do your sisters forbid their servants to smile?"

"Servants?" Tom said in surprise. "Do you think my sisters have *servants?*"

"Of course," replied Edward. "Who else helps your sisters to get dressed in the morning?"

"No one, sir," replied Tom. "They each sleep in their dress. So they are already clothed when they wake."

"Their dress?" asked the prince. "Do they have just one each?"

"Naturally," said Tom. "After all, they each have only one body. What would they do with more clothes?"

The prince laughed. "Well said! But Nan and Bet shall have plenty of clothes and servants soon. I will see to it," he promised. "You speak well, Tom. Who has taught you?"

"The good priest Father Andrew, from his books," Tom explained.

"Tell me about Offal Court," said the prince. "Do you have a pleasant time?"

"Oh, yes, sir!" exclaimed Tom. "Unless we are hungry. All the children there run races. And in the summer we swim in the river."

The prince sighed longingly. "It would be worth my father's kingdom if I could play like that! But go on."

"We play in the sand—and sometimes make mud and wallow in it," Tom said. "It is most delightful, sir!"

"Oh, say no more!" said Edward. "If I could only put on ragged clothing like yours and wallow in the mud—just once—with no one to scold me...I would give up the crown I wear!"

Tom's eyes grew wide. "And if I could only put on clothes like yours—"

The prince clapped his hands gleefully. "Then let us do so!" he cried.

A few minutes later, the Prince of Wales was wearing Tom's rags. And Tom had put on the prince's fancy clothing. They stood side by side and gazed at themselves in a large mirror.

But it did not look as if they had exchanged clothes at all! It was almost impossible to tell the difference between the prince and the pauper.

"Look—we have the same hair, the same eyes, the same face!" Edward exclaimed. "And we're the same size!"

The two boys stared at the mirror in

silence. Then Edward noticed one difference between them. There was a bruise on Tom's hand.

"That soldier outside hurt you!" the prince cried angrily. He stamped his bare foot. "How cruel!"

In an instant, he grabbed something that was lying on the table and put it away. Then he ran out of the room. "Do not move until I return!" he shouted back to Tom.

The prince raced down to the palace gates in Tom's tattered clothing and grabbed the bars. "Open up!" he cried.

The soldier obeyed at once. But when Edward burst through the gate, the soldier sent him sprawling on the roadway.

"Take that, you beggar!" the soldier said with a mean laugh. He did not realize the boy was really the prince!

The people in the street roared with laughter. None of them recognized Edward, either.

The prince picked himself up. "I am the Prince of Wales!" he declared. "You shall be punished for hitting me!"

"I salute Your Highness!" the soldier said mockingly as he raised his sword.

Then he sneered. "Be off, crazy boy!"

The jeering crowd of people pushed the ragged prince down the road, away from the palace gates. "Make way for His Royal Highness!" they hooted. "Make way for the royal Prince of Wales!"

Chapter Three
The Prince's Troubles Begin

The mob chased and teased the prince for hours. When they finally left him alone, the prince's feet were bleeding. And he was hopelessly lost.

After walking aimlessly for another hour, he came upon a group of boys playing in a churchyard. Edward suddenly felt hopeful. His father had turned this church into a place that clothed and fed poor orphans. Surely these boys would help the king's son!

"Good lads, tell your master that the Prince of Wales wishes to speak with him," the prince commanded.

"And who are you—the prince's messenger?" a boy asked rudely.

"I am the prince himself!" declared Edward. The boys hooted with laughter. This beggar boy a prince? Before Edward could stop them, the lads set dogs upon him and chased him away.

11

As he fled through the streets, Edward wondered at the cruelty of the boys. "Their stomachs are full, for they have enough to eat," he thought. "But their minds are starved!

"When I am king, they shall have books to learn from," he vowed. "For learning can help a person become gentle and kind."

As night approached, Edward found himself with bleeding hands and a bruised body. His ragged clothes were covered with mud.

He wandered on and on, so tired he could hardly drag his feet. People in the streets paid no attention to him.

"Offal Court," the prince muttered as he trudged along. "That is where Tom lives. If I can find it, I am saved! His family will take me to the palace and prove that I am the true prince."

A gusty wind blew, and it began to rain. Suddenly a large man jumped out of a dark alley and grabbed Edward.

"It is already nightfall," hissed the man, "and I wager that you have not brought home a single penny! I will punish you—as sure as my name is John Canty!"

The prince twisted himself loose. "You are Tom's father!" he exclaimed eagerly. "I am hurt and tired. Take me to the king, my father. He will make you rich beyond your dreams! Believe me, for I speak the truth—I am indeed the Prince of Wales!"

The man stared down at the boy. "You have gone mad!" he said. He grasped Edward by the collar and declared, "Mad or not, you shall be punished!"

And with that, he dragged the struggling prince up the street. A noisy mob began to follow them.

"Let me go!" shouted the prince. He tried to pull away as John Canty raised a thick stick.

"Do not hit the boy!" pleaded an old man standing nearby. He rushed between John and Edward—and the stick struck the man on the head!

The man groaned and sank down to the pavement. But the crowd ignored him. They were too busy watching John Canty drag Edward away.

The rest of the Canty family gaped when Edward and John Canty arrived at the house in Offal Court.

A dim candle lit the dirty room. Edward shuddered as a mean-looking old woman with lank gray hair stole out from a corner. Another woman and two ragged girls crouched against a wall.

"Say your name again, lad!" ordered John Canty.

"I will tell you now as I told you before," Edward said firmly. "I am Edward, Prince of Wales."

John Canty laughed coarsely. Tom's grandmother just looked amazed. But Tom's mother and sisters ran over to Edward.

Tears rose in the mother's eyes. "Oh, Tom, my poor boy!" she said. "You have lost your wits from all that reading!"

Edward smiled and said gently, "Your son is well and has not lost his wits. Take me to the palace. There the king—my father—will give you your son."

"Oh, Tom!" the mother cried. "Wake up from your royal dreams! Look at me. Am I not your mother, who loves you?"

The prince sadly shook his head. "Truly, I have never seen you before," he declared.

Tom's mother sobbed loudly. His father glared at Edward. "What money did you get from begging today?" he asked angrily.

"I have not begged today. I tell you, I am the king's son!" insisted Edward.

"Enough of this nonsense! You shall have no supper, my boy. Now go to bed—all of you!" shouted John Canty.

In a short time, Tom's father and grandmother fell asleep. Then Nan and Bet crept over to Edward. They lovingly covered him with straw and rags to keep him warm.

Their mother came over, too. She stroked Edward's hair and gave him some morsels of bread to eat.

"Thank you for your kindness," Edward whispered to her. "My father, the king, will surely reward you."

Tom's mother went back to bed. But she could not sleep. Had her son lost his mind? What if the boy really was not her son? She almost smiled at the thought. But she could not stop wondering.

Then she had an idea. A simple test would put her mind to rest and prove that he was her son.

"Tom raises his hands if he wakes suddenly," Tom's mother thought. "But with his palms facing outward, not toward his face like others. I have seen it happen many times!"

She took her lit candle and crept over to Edward, who was now sleeping. Then she flashed the light on his face and rapped on the floor near his ear.

Edward's eyes popped open. He looked around in alarm. But he made no special movement with his hands.

Tom's mother did not know what to think. She soothed the boy back to sleep and tried the test again and again. But each time, Edward reacted the same way.

Confused, she crawled back to bed.

"But he must be my son!" she sobbed silently. Hours passed, and Edward slept heavily. He woke at the sound of shouting in the street. Then there were sharp knocks on the door.

John Canty woke and hissed, "Who is there? What do you want?"

A voice answered. "Do you know who you hit last night in the street?"

"No—and I don't care, either," snarled John Canty.

"The man was Father Andrew, the priest," said the voice at the door. "And he is dead!"

"Mercy!" cried John Canty. Quickly, he woke his family. "Up with you all and flee!" he ordered hoarsely.

In five minutes, the Cantys were out in the dark street and running for their lives. John Canty held the prince by the wrist and hurried him along.

"Watch your tongue and do not tell our name to anyone," he whispered to Edward.

To the rest of his family, he added, "If we become separated, go to London Bridge. We will meet up there."

As he spoke, the group turned a corner into a blaze of light. Crowds of people were singing, dancing, and shouting along the Thames River. Bonfires blazed everywhere, and colorful lanterns hung on barges. Noisy fireworks exploded in the night sky.

In an instant, the Cantys were swallowed up by the celebrating crowds and separated from one another. But John Canty kept his grip on the prince.

"Take a drink!" a burly man insisted loudly. "In honor of the Prince of Wales!" He thrust a huge cup at John Canty. Tom's father grasped the cup with one hand and used his other hand to lift the cup's lid.

This left the prince's wrist free for a moment. Without wasting a second, he ran off and disappeared among the crowds of people.

Chapter Four

Tom at the Palace

While Edward Tudor was living the life of a pauper, Tom Canty was living the life of a prince!

At first, when the prince ran out of the room after changing into Tom's clothes, Tom waited for him to return.

He admired himself in the grand mirror. What would the people in Offal Court say if they could see Tom here in royal clothes? Would they even believe his tale when he returned home?

After half an hour, Tom began to wonder what had happened to his new friend. He felt lonely—and worried, too.

Suppose someone came in and found Tom wearing these clothes! And the prince would not be there to explain why. Would they punish Tom by hanging him?

He paced the room nervously. Suddenly the door swung open. A page stepped into the room and announced, "The lady Jane Grey."

A young girl in a beautiful dress ran over to Tom. But she stopped when she saw his sad face. "What ails you, my lord?" she asked sweetly.

"I beg for mercy. I am no lord, just poor Tom Canty of Offal Court," Tom stammered. "Please allow me to see the prince. He will give me back my rags and let me leave." He knelt down. "Save me!" he pleaded.

Lady Jane looked horrified. "Oh, my lord! You bow—to *me*?" She ran off, and Tom sank to the floor in despair.

As he lay there, word spread through the palace. "The prince has gone mad! The prince has gone mad!"

A few minutes later, there was a buzz in the hallways. "The prince! See, the prince comes!"

Tom walked slowly past bowing lords and ladies, servants and common folk. He meekly gazed around at his strange surroundings. A lord walked on each side of Tom to support him.

The lords led Tom to an elegant room in the palace. There sat a very large man with a very stern expression. His legs were swollen, and one of them was bandaged and rested on a pillow.

This ill man was Edward's father, King Henry VIII. He could be harsh to his subjects and was feared by many. But he was always kind to his son.

The king's face grew gentle as he spoke. "How are you, Edward? Are you playing a jest on me, the good king your father, who loves you?"

Tom dropped to his knees. "You are the *king?* Then I am in trouble indeed!"

Tom's words stunned the king. "Alas, I fear the rumors are true," he said sadly. He sighed. "Come to your father. You do know me, do you not?"

"Yes, you are the king," Tom said, trembling. "But I am too young to die. A word from you will save me from a hanging."

"Die?" asked the king. "Do not talk so! Of course you shall not die."

"Oh, mercy, thank you!" cried Tom. "Now will you set me free?"

The king was puzzled. Had his son truly gone mad? He decided to test him.

He asked Tom a question in Latin. And Tom slowly answered! The king was delighted.

Then he asked Tom a question in

21

French. "I do not know that language, Your Majesty," Tom replied.

The king turned to address the other people in the room. His gentle manner had changed. "Too much studying has done this to him!" he declared. "Take away his books and teachers. Let him rest instead, until he is well. He may be mad, but he is still my son. And he will rule after me!"

Tom was escorted from the room. His heart was sad. Would he ever be able to go home? Or would he remain a captive in the palace? Being a prince was not as pleasant as he had imagined.

Tom was taken to an elegant set of rooms and given a chair to sit in. Old men and nobles stood around him, and Tom begged them to sit down, too. But they only bowed, thanked him, and remained standing.

Lord Hertford whispered to Tom, "Do not insist, my lord. It is not right that they sit in your presence." Then he showed Tom how to dismiss everyone from the room.

The lord then spoke privately to Tom. "His Majesty the king commands that the prince shall hide his illness till he be well again. He shall not deny that he is the true prince. He will not speak of his lowly life, which he imagines. If he does not know what to say or do, he shall take my advice."

"The king shall be obeyed," said Tom. He knew he had no choice.

"Now ease yourself with entertainment," said Lord Hertford. "Then you will not be weary at the city's grand banquet tonight."

Soon the prince's sister Princess Elizabeth arrived. The prince's cousin Lady Jane Grey was with her. Tom remembered that Edward was fond of these two girls.

But he found their visit difficult at first. Lady Jane asked questions that he could not answer.

"Have you paid a visit to the queen today?" she asked Tom.

Tom did not know how to reply to her questions. One question was even in Greek! But Princess Elizabeth was kind. She answered for Tom when she saw he was confused.

So the visit passed pleasantly enough, and Tom grew more at ease. He had been worried about the banquet. But it turned out that the two girls would be going, too.

That made Tom feel a little better. They were not strangers to him anymore.

By and by, Tom was taken to a room to rest. But he could not sleep. His mind was too full of thoughts, and the room was too full of servants.

Meanwhile, Lord Hertford wondered to himself if two boys could look so alike. It would not be strange if an ordinary lad claimed to *be* the prince. But this boy claimed he was not.

There was only one explanation. This must be the true prince, gone mad!

In the afternoon, Tom ate a large meal by himself at a heavy gold table. A servant tied a dainty napkin around Tom's neck. Another servant poured him a glass of wine. A third servant stood ready to taste any dish, in case it was poisoned!

Tom picked up the food with his fingers. He had no idea how to use the many forks and knives. In fact, he had never used silverware. But no one smiled at Tom's behavior. The servants had been told not to show surprise.

Tom pointed to the napkin. He did not know what it was for, either. "Please take this away," he said politely. "Otherwise, my fingers might soil it!"

He looked at the vegetables, which were new to him. "Are these to be eaten?" he asked.

"Yes, Your Majesty. They are turnips and lettuce," explained one of the lords who stood nearby. "We now grow them here in England."

At the end of the meal, Tom filled his pockets with nuts to munch on later. Then a lord came over with a shallow gold dish. In it was sweet-smelling rose water to clean Tom's mouth and fingers.

But Tom did not know what the water was for. First he gazed at the dish, puzzled. Then he raised it to his lips and took a sip. "Nay, I do not like it, my lord," he stated. "It tastes pretty, but it is weak."

Everyone in the room was saddened to see the prince drink the rose water. The prince's mind was clearly ruined!

After being taken back to his room, Tom was finally left alone. He spied pieces of shining armor hanging on hooks. Wearing them was tempting! Tom tried on as many pieces as he could without help.

Then he remembered the nuts from

dinner. He put away the armor and was soon happily cracking nuts. How wonderful to eat with no servants looking on!

Then Tom found some books in a closet. One was about manners in the English royal court. He lay down on the sofa and began to read. The book was full of things to learn.

Around five o'clock, Lord Hertford came looking for the Great Seal. It was a large stamp used on the king's official papers. But Tom did not know that.

"The king gave the Great Seal to you just two days ago," Lord Hertford said to Tom.

"I do not recall that," Tom said. In fact, he had not been in the palace two days ago! But he knew it was useless to explain that to the lord.

Lord Hertford went to King Henry VIII and told him what Tom had said. The king sighed.

"Trouble the poor child no more," he said. "Since the Great Seal is missing, I will use the Small Seal instead. Bring it here!"

By nine o'clock that evening, the river blazed with lights from colored lanterns.

Boats and barges filled the water.

A row of forty state barges drew up to the stone steps behind the palace. Some barges were decorated with banners and streamers. Others had silk flags hung with tiny silver bells.

Two rows of guards lined the steps leading down to the water. A grand parade of lords and officers walked between them. Then came a blast of trumpets.

"Make way for the high and mighty, the lord Edward, Prince of Wales!"

Tom Canty stepped into view and bowed his head slightly. He wore a white satin doublet. The front of the outfit was purple cloth covered with diamonds. His cape was set with pearls and jewels, and lined in blue satin.

The crowd welcomed him with a roar of happiness. What a greeting for a boy who was used to dirt and rags!

Chapter Five
The Prince Meets Miles Hendon

Tom boarded the royal barge and sailed in state down the Thames River. He was headed toward the Guildhall for a royal banquet. Princess Elizabeth and Lady Jane were at his side.

At the same time, the real prince was in a rush. He had escaped from Tom's father in the crowded streets. But Edward quickly realized two things.

One, it would be impossible for John Canty to find him. And two, the city of London was honoring a fake prince! It must be the pauper lad, Tom Canty, pretending to be the Prince of Wales! There was only one thing Edward could do. He would have to go to the Guildhall and make himself known as the real prince!

When Tom and his new friends arrived at the Guildhall, they were welcomed by the lord mayor. Then the grand banquet began.

Everyone in the room took a turn

drinking from a large golden loving cup. Platters of roast beef were served. A procession of dukes, earls, and barons filed past Tom. Each was dressed in magnificent clothes. Lords and ladies sang and danced to provide entertainment.

While all this was going on inside, the ragged but real Prince of Wales had reached the Guildhall. He insisted on being let indoors. The throngs of people in the street laughed at hearing the boy's proclamations.

"I tell you again, I am the Prince of Wales!" Edward exclaimed. "I may not have friends, but I will not be driven away from here!" Tears came to his eyes as the mob mocked him.

Suddenly a tall man spoke up. "You may or may not be a prince. But you are a gallant lad, with a friend. And here I—Miles Hendon—am by your side to prove it!"

The speaker's clothing was of rich material, but faded and worn. The feather in his hat was broken, and he wore a long sword by his side.

The crowd jeered at Miles. "Throw the boy in the pond!" they cried.

A man in the crowd reached out to grab

Edward. Instantly Miles knocked the man to the ground with his sword.

The next moment voices shouted, "Kill the dog! Kill the dog!" The mob closed around Miles. He backed against a wall and began to fight with his long sword. But he was only one man against many. How could he win?

Suddenly a trumpet blast sounded.

"Make way for the king's messenger!" came the cry. A troop of riders on horses charged down on the people, who fled for their lives!

The bold stranger quickly caught the prince up in his arms and ran swiftly down the road. They were soon far away from danger and the crowd.

Inside the Guildhall, a single bugle note was blown. At once there was silence in the huge hall.

The messenger from the palace gave his announcement: "The king is dead!"

All the people bowed their heads in prayer for a few moments. Then they sank to their knees and stretched their hands out to Tom.

A mighty shout burst forth. It almost

shook the building. "Long live the king!"

Tom's eyes were dazed as he looked at the people bowing to him. Then he had a thought. He turned to Lord Hertford.

"Tell me the truth," Tom whispered. "If I give a command, will it be obeyed?"

"You are the king of England now," replied the earl. "Your word is law."

Tom spoke up loudly. "The king's law shall be one of mercy and kindness from this day on!"

The good news spread throughout the hall. "Long live Edward, king of England!"

Chapter Six
"Long Live the King!"

Miles Hendon and Edward made their way through the mob and headed toward the river. Miles kept a firm grip on Edward's wrist. He did not want to risk losing the boy.

The crowd grew again as they reached London Bridge. The news had already spread, and Edward heard it from many voices: "The king is dead!"

The boy shuddered at the news. He felt a great sadness. His father, King Henry VIII, was a terror to many. But he had always been gentle with Edward.

Then he heard more cries. "Long live King Edward the Sixth!" The boy's heart swelled with pride.

"How grand and strange it seems—*I am king!*" he thought.

London Bridge linked the cities of London and Southwark. The bridge was almost a town itself. On it were bakeries, hat shops, food markets—even a church. Families lived above the stores. And everyone knew each other.

Miles was staying in the little inn on the bridge. As he neared the door with his new friend, a harsh voice spoke. It was John Canty!

"So you've come back at last! Well, you'll not escape another time," he said. He put out his hand to grab Edward.

Miles stepped between them. "Not so fast!" he said. "What is the boy to you?"

"None of your business—but he is my son," said John Canty.

"That is a lie!" Edward protested. "I do not know him. And I will not go with him."

"Boldly said, and I believe you," Miles said kindly. He tapped his sword hilt and turned to John Canty. "Do not touch him! Even if you are his father, I will not leave him in your brute care!"

John Canty moved off, muttering threats and curses.

Miles asked the innkeeper to send them some food. Then he took Edward up three flights of stairs. Two candles dimly lit his shabby room.

It was now two o'clock in the morning. The exhausted young king dragged himself to the bed.

"Call me when the meal is ready," he murmured, and fell asleep at once.

Miles pitied Edward. The poor lad thought he was the Prince of Wales! Yet Miles admired the boy, too. For Edward had stood up like a brave soldier to the crowd's taunts.

"I will care for him and watch over him as a brother," Miles thought. "And I will cure his madness!"

He paced around the cold room and made plans. He would take Edward with him to visit Miles's family. It had been ten long years since he had last been to Hendon Hall. But surely Miles's father would welcome them both.

Edward woke suddenly when a servant brought up a hot meal. He looked around, and his face grew sad.

"Alas, it was just a dream," he said with a deep sigh.

Then Edward walked over to the washstand in the corner. "Good sir, I would wash," he said to Miles.

"You are welcome to," Miles replied.

But the boy simply stood and waited. He tapped the floor with his foot once or twice.

"Bless us, what is it?" Miles asked.

"Pour the water and do not talk so much!" ordered the boy.

Miles stifled a laugh and did as Edward had commanded.

"Come, the towel!" came the next kingly order. The towel was right in front of Edward. But Miles handed it to him anyway.

Edward sat down at the table and began to eat. When Miles finished his own washing, he went to sit down in the other chair.

"Stop!" warned Edward. "How dare you sit in the presence of a king?"

Miles was taken by surprise. "The poor lad's madness is up to date!" he said to himself. "In his mind, he is now *king!* I must go along with it...or he will send me to the Tower to be hung!"

He was pleased by his little joke and stood up. Then he waited on the king in the most courtly way he could.

Warmed by the supper, Edward soon began to talk.

"You have a gallant way about you," he

said to Miles. "Tell me your story. Are you from a noble family?"

"Yes, Your Majesty," said Miles. "My father is a baronet, rich yet generous. My older brother, Arthur, is also goodhearted. But my younger brother, Hugh, has always been mean and cruel."

Miles then went on to explain how he had been in love with his cousin, the lady Edith. And she loved Miles in return. But she was betrothed to Arthur. And Miles's father would not allow the marriage contract to be broken.

"Hugh loved Edith, too—or rather, he loved her wealth," Miles added. "Arthur was not healthy. And Hugh wanted me gone. So he convinced my father that I planned to elope with Edith and marry her against my father's wishes.

"My father was angry and banished me from England for three years. He said it would make a soldier and a man of me. It did, for I fought bravely in the Continental wars. But in my last battle I was taken captive!"

Miles explained that he was jailed in a foreign dungeon for seven long years. His courage helped him to escape at last.

"I fled here straightaway," he told Edward. "I am poor in money and clothing. And I do not know what has happened in the past seven years to my family or Hendon Hall."

"You have been treated badly!" said Edward, his eyes flashing in anger. "But I will make it right—the king has said it!" He then told Miles his own tale.

When Edward had finished, Miles said to himself, "What an imagination the boy has! Well, he shall not lack for a friend while I am alive!"

Edward then spoke up thoughtfully. "You saved me from injury and shame—in fact, you saved my life and thus the royal crown! Such service deserves rich reward. Name your wish, and if I have the power to grant it, I shall."

Miles knelt down and said, "I beg the king to grant me one privilege—that I and my heirs may *sit* in the presence of the majesty of England!"

Edward gently tapped Miles on the shoulder with the sword. "Rise, Sir Miles, and seat yourself," said Edward gravely. "I name you a knight. Your wish is granted."

Miles gratefully dropped into a chair.

His legs were weary from standing. "How fortunate I thought to ask for this," he mused to himself. "Otherwise, I might have stood for weeks, until the lad's wits were cured!"

Edward soon became drowsy. He lay down on the bed again. Miles tucked the blankets around the boy.

"You will sleep in front of the door and guard it," Edward ordered. A moment later, he was slumbering.

"He should have been born a king!" muttered Miles in admiration. "He plays the part so well."

Then he stretched out in front of the door. "I have had worse beds than this floor in seven years," he thought, and fell asleep as dawn arrived.

At noon, Miles awoke and opened the door to go out.

The noise woke Edward. "What are you doing?" he murmured.

"I have an errand to do," Miles replied. "But I will soon return."

Thirty minutes later, Miles came back. He carried a boy's suit, secondhand and worn in places. Still, it was tidy and better than Edward's rags.

Miles took out a needle and thread. He carefully mended the rips in the garment. As he worked, he softly hummed a tune. He did not want to wake the sleeping boy.

At last, the mending was done. Miles was pleased with his handiwork. "Now I will wake the boy and help him to dress and eat. Then we will be on our way to Hendon Hall."

He went over to the bed. "My lord!" he called, but there was no answer. He threw back the covers. But the boy was *gone!*

Miles shouted for the innkeeper. At that moment, a servant entered with breakfast.

"Where is the boy?" raged Miles.

"After you went out, a youth came running in," stammered the frightened servant. "He said you wanted the boy brought to you at the Southwark end of the bridge.

"The youth gave the lad the message," the servant continued. "The boy grumbled at being woken. But he went off with the youth."

"You are a fool!" cried Miles. "But perhaps no harm is meant. I will go fetch him." He looked at the bed. "Wait! When I returned earlier, the bed looked as though someone were in it. How did that happen?"

"I do not know, sir. But I saw the youth meddle with the blankets," the servant said nervously.

"Oh, no! It was done to trick me!" Miles said angrily. "Was that youth alone? Take your time and think, man!"

"He came alone," said the servant. "But as he and the lad stepped into the crowd, a ruffian man joined them—"

"What then?" interrupted Miles.

"I lost sight of them quickly. But they headed toward Southwark."

Miles plunged down the stairs, two steps at a time. He knew who the ruffian was. It must have been John Canty!

"That scurvy villain! He claimed Edward was his son!" Miles muttered. His heart ached at the thought of the missing boy. "You may be lost, my child—but I will ransack the land until I find you!"

Chapter Seven

Tom as King

That same morning, Tom Canty lay in bed, dreaming pleasantly of playing in a field. Suddenly a dwarf appeared in his dream and said, "Dig by that stump."

Tom did so and found twelve shiny new pennies!

"Dig here every seven days, and you will always find the same treasure," the dwarf said. Then he vanished.

Tom ran home to Offal Court. "Every night, I will give my father a penny," Tom said to himself. "He will be happy and no longer punish me! I will give one penny each week to the kind priest. The other four pennies I will give to my mother and sisters. No more hunger and rags and fears!"

He reached his home out of breath. Throwing four pennies into his mother's lap, he cried, "They are for you and Nan and Bet! And I got them honestly—not by begging or stealing!"

His happy mother clasped Tom in her arms and exclaimed, "It is getting late. May it please Your Majesty to rise?"

That was not what Tom expected to hear. The dream stopped as he awoke.

A cluster of noble servants stood in his bedroom. The memory of the glad dream faded away. Tom was still a captive and a king.

Fourteen noble servants helped Tom to dress in his royal clothes. Starting with a shirt, one piece of clothing at a time was passed down a line until it reached the young king. It reminded Tom of passing buckets of water at a fire!

Then Tom was taken to breakfast. As he passed by the masses of courtly people, they dropped to their knees and bowed.

After breakfast, Tom went to the throne room. State business was conducted there. Lord Hertford stood by Tom's side to assist him in his new role as king.

A secretary stepped forward. He read a document listing the expenses of King Henry VIII's household. Tom gasped when he heard the huge amounts of money.

However, there was hardly any money

left in the royal coffers. The twelve hundred servants were not going to be paid their wages.

Tom had heard enough. He had to speak his mind. "We must move to a smaller house and get rid of the servants," he said firmly. "I know of a small house near the fish market—"

A sharp push on Tom's arm made him stop. He blushed at his foolishness. A king would not let servants go! What was he thinking?

As the morning wore on, Tom gave his approval to various matters. People were named earls and dukes. Money and land were granted to them.

Then Tom had a happy thought. He could name his mother duchess of Offal Court and give her money and land of her own!

Suddenly he remembered—he was not really a king at all. So he kept the idea to himself.

More papers and proclamations were read. Tom's poor head became so muddled! The work finally ended when Tom fell asleep.

In the afternoon, Tom had some time to himself. A twelve-year-old boy came to see him. The boy was dressed all in black, except for a white ruff around his neck and lace at his wrists. He dropped to one knee and bowed his head.

"Rise, lad," commanded Tom. "Who are you? What do you want?"

"Surely you remember me, my lord," said the boy. "I am Humphrey Marlow, your whipping boy."

Tom had never heard of a whipping boy. But he thought quickly. "I seem to remember you somewhat," he began. "But my memory is clogged and dim. Sometimes a clue helps me."

"Two days ago, you made a mistake in your lessons," Humphrey reminded him. "Your teacher was angry at your laziness. He vowed to whip me."

"Whip *you*?" asked Tom in amazement. "Why whip you for faults that are mine?"

"No one may hit the Prince of Wales," explained Humphrey. "So I take the whipping for you. It is my job."

Tom marveled at this idea. Then the boy spoke again. He sounded worried.

"Since you are now king, you will no longer have dreary schoolwork," Humphrey said. "There will be no need for me. And I and my orphan sisters will surely starve!"

Tom assured him that would not happen. "I will study my books so poorly that you will be paid extra!" he promised Humphrey.

He encouraged the boy to talk. Humphrey was glad to do so. He believed he was helping to cure the king's memory.

Humphrey reminded Tom of adventures in the schoolroom and palace. And one by one, Tom "remembered" them.

At the end of an hour, Tom was full of information about people and customs in the royal court.

After Humphrey left, Lord Hertford came in. He informed Tom that he would have to start dining in public soon. The court wanted to stop any gossip about the king's health from spreading.

Tom's memory seemed much improved. Lord Hertford was pleased to see this. So he asked Tom once more about the Great Seal.

"Your father, the late king, needed it

yesterday," Lord Hertford reminded him.

Tom was at a loss. "What did it look like?" he asked innocently.

Lord Hertford was shaken. The boy's wits had flown again!

The next day, Tom received foreign ambassadors. He enjoyed the splendor of their colorful robes, but their long speeches became dreary. He was glad when the ceremony was over.

Once again, he spent a private hour talking with Humphrey Marlow. The time was useful, as Tom was entertained and informed.

By Tom's third day as king, he started to feel a little more comfortable in his royal role. And he was growing used to his fancy surroundings.

The fourth day quickly arrived. This was the one Tom dreaded: he was going to dine in public later that afternoon. Hundreds of eyes would be looking at him, watching for any mistakes!

Once again, the royal duties in the morning were tiring. In the afternoon, Tom waited for a meeting. Bored, he wandered over to the window and looked out.

A mob of poor people was approaching from the road below. The men, women, and children were hooting and shouting noisily.

"I would know what it is about!" Tom commanded an earl.

A messenger soon told Tom that the mob was following a man, woman, and girl who were criminals. The three were on their way to be hung.

Tom was horrified. He did not stop to think about the crimes the three people supposedly had committed. Instead, he ordered them to be brought to him.

First, the doomed man knelt before Tom. He looked familiar.

"This is the stranger who plucked Giles Watt out of the river last New Year's Day," Tom said to himself. "It was ten in the morning, a windy, bitter day—and he saved Giles's life! It was a brave and good deed."

Tom turned to the sheriff. "What is this prisoner's offense?" he asked.

"Your Majesty, he poisoned a man," replied the sheriff. "It was clearly proven at the trial."

Tom sighed and said, "The prisoner has earned his death. It is a pity, for he was a brave—I mean, he *looks* brave!"

The prisoner clasped his hands in despair. "Oh, my lord!" he begged Tom. "Have pity on me, for I am innocent!"

"Good sir, I wish to look into this further," Tom said to the sheriff. "Tell me what you know about this case."

"Witnesses say this man entered a sick man's house in Islington at ten in the morning," the sheriff said. "The sick man was alone and sleeping. This man soon came out. The sick man died within an hour. His symptoms all pointed to poison.

"There is more, Your Majesty," the sheriff continued. "Many in the village say that a witch told them that the sick man would die by poison. The witch also said that a stranger with brown hair and old clothing would give the poison to him. The witch has since left the village, and none know where she is. But this criminal has brown hair, and his clothing is worn!"

Tom felt he had to give the accused man one more chance to defend himself. "Speak up," Tom said to the man.

"I have no friends," the man began. "If so, they could tell you I was not in Islington. In fact, when the sick man was poisoned, I was miles away at the Thames River.

"They say I was taking a life at that hour, but I actually saved one!" added the man. "A drowning boy—"

"Sheriff, name the day the crime was done!" cried Tom.

"On the first day of the new year," the sheriff answered. That was when Giles had been saved. And it was all Tom needed to hear. The man was innocent!

"Let the prisoner go!" proclaimed Tom. "It is the king's will! It angers me that a man should be hanged because of such harebrained evidence!"

The crowd of courtiers buzzed with admiration. They liked Tom's wit and spirit. "This is no mad king," they said among themselves. "His wits are strong! His questions were sane!"

Next, Tom summoned the other two prisoners. The sobbing woman and girl were brought into the room.

"What have they done?" Tom asked.

"Please Your Majesty, they have sold their souls to the devil," said the sheriff.

Tom shuddered to hear of this wicked-
ness. But he was also curious. "What is your
proof?" he asked.

"The devil gave them power, and they
used it to cause a fierce storm," the sheriff
explained. "Forty people lost their homes."

Tom thought about this. "Did the
woman also suffer from the storm?"

"Indeed, Your Majesty," the sheriff
answered. "She and the child were left
without their home."

"So she herself paid a heavy price for
this power," Tom pointed out. "That shows
that she is mad. And if she was mad, she
did not know what she was doing. There-
fore, she is not at fault."

The noblemen in the room nodded.
They agreed with Tom's wisdom.

But Tom was still curious. "How did the
two cause the storm?" he asked.

"By pulling off their stockings, Sire."

"How wonderful!" Tom exclaimed. He
turned to the woman. "Use your power—I
want to see a storm! Do not worry; I will
not blame you for it. In fact, if you can do
this, you and your child will be freed and
no one will harm you."

The terrified woman looked puzzled.

"Oh, my lord, I have been wrongly accused! I do not have such power."

Tom urged again. But the woman insisted she could not create even a small storm.

"If I could do such a miracle upon your command, I gladly would. I would even give up my own life for that of my child," she said tearfully.

Tom declared, "The woman speaks the truth, I believe! Any mother would call up a storm and ruin the land if it meant the saving of her child's life.

"You are both innocent!" he said to the woman and her daughter, and sent the grateful pair on their way.

After his experiences in the morning and early afternoon, Tom was more confident. Yet he was still worried about dining in public.

The banquet room was enormous. Paintings decorated the walls and ceiling. Tall guards stood by the door, as still as statues.

A high balcony ringed the room. It was packed with musicians and brightly dressed citizens. A table on a raised platform sat in the center of the room. This was where Tom would dine.

The assembly heard the blast of a bugle. Then came the cry, "Make way for the king!" A long procession of noble lords and ladies marched in first.

Then trumpets and drums saluted Tom's entrance. He nodded to the welcoming crowd. "I thank you, my good people," he said politely.

Once he was seated at the table, courses were served. Guards tasted each dish first, to make sure they were not poisoned.

Hundreds of eyes watched Tom eat his dinner, bite by bite. Tom was careful not to hurry. He also did not do anything for himself but waited for the proper official to perform the task.

When the meal was over, Tom marched away triumphantly. For he had gotten through the dinner without making a single mistake.

Chapter Eight
Foo-foo the First

Three days before Tom's public dinner, Miles Hendon hurried along London Bridge. He was searching for the youth who had taken Edward from the inn.

But Miles had no luck. He could not find them—or John Canty—anywhere. He decided to stick to his original plan and head to Hendon Hall. He was sure that Edward, if he could, would go there to seek Miles.

Meanwhile, the youth rushed Edward along, telling him that Miles lay wounded in a forest. John Canty followed behind, unseen by Edward.

"Miles wounded? Who dared to do that? Lead me there!" ordered Edward.

The youth took Edward to a deserted and decaying barn in the woods.

Miles was not there. But a fellow who Edward realized had been following them appeared. He wore a green eye patch and walked with a cane. One arm was in a sling.

"Who are you?" Edward asked him.

"My disguise is good," said the ruffian. "But surely you can tell I am your father— John Canty!"

"You are not my father," insisted Edward. "I am the king."

"It is plain you are mad," John Canty said sternly. "Where are your mother and sisters? Do you know where they went?"

"Don't ask me such questions," said the king angrily. "My mother is dead. My sisters are in the palace."

The youth who had led Edward to the barn laughed. "Peace, Hugo," John Canty said to him. "The boy's mind is wandering. But I need his service."

Canty and Hugo started talking softly to each other. Edward went to the far end of the barn. There he lay down on a thick pile of straw. He was exhausted and missed his real father terribly. He soon fell asleep.

The sound of coarse laughter woke him. A bright fire burned on the floor at the other end of the barn. Around the fire sat tattered tramps and thieves, both men and women.

Edward listened to their rough talk. It turned out that John Canty used to be part of this group. Their chief was known as the Ruffler, and he greeted Canty warmly. The Ruffler told him what the group had been doing lately.

Some of the men took off their rags. They showed Canty the welts on their backs from beatings. Another man was missing an ear.

Edward listened to their ghastly tales from his straw bed. One man had been killed in a brawl. A woman had a gift for telling fortunes, but she was called a witch for it and roasted alive! Others lost their homes when their farms were turned into sheep ranges.

"I was once a farmer but fell on hard times. I was sold as a slave," one man said bitterly. "I ran away. But if my master finds me, I shall be hung! It is the law of the land."

"You shall not!" rang out a voice. "That law has ended as of this day!"

The tramps turned and saw Edward. "Who is this?" they asked in surprise.

"I am Edward, king of England."

The tramps laughed. Edward was angry. Why weren't they grateful?

"He is my son, a dreamer and a mad

fool!" said Canty. "Do not mind him—he thinks he *is* the king."

"You will soon know that I *am* the king," Edward said to him. "You murdered a man. For that, you will hang!"

"You'll betray me?" shouted Canty.

"Tut-tut!" said the Ruffler. He knocked Canty aside, saying, "Have some respect for kings and Rufflers!"

Then he turned to Edward. "Do not threaten us, lad. We are your mates. We may be bad in some ways. But none of us would betray the king. So pretend to be king if you wish, but do not call yourself one."

"Long live Edward, king of England!" cried the tramps.

Edward's face lit up. "I thank you, my good people," he said.

The crew burst into merry laughter again. "I tell you again, drop the title of king," the Ruffler urged him. "You sound like a traitor, and it is not wise to use it. Choose another."

"Foo-foo the First, king of the Moon-calves!" shrieked a tinker.

A roar went up. "Long live Foo-foo the

First, king of the Mooncalves!" This was followed by catcalls and hooting.

"Crown him! Robe him! Scepter him! Throne him!"

Moments later, poor Edward was crowned with a tin basin. He was robed in a tattered blanket and seated on a barrel for a throne. An iron rod became his scepter.

Then the group bowed down to him. "Be gracious to us, O sweet King!" they hooted merrily.

Edward's eyes filled with tears. He was both ashamed and angry. He had tried to be kind—and this was how they treated him!

Chapter Nine
The Prince and the Tramps

The outlaws set out early the next day. The sky was stormy, and the ground was muddy. A chill was in the winter air.

The Ruffler felt that Edward could be useful to the gang in some way. He put Hugo in charge of the boy and warned the man not to be too rough with him. He also ordered John Canty to keep away from Edward.

As the day wore on, the troop grew more cheerful. They insulted people along the road. They stole linen that was draped on hedges.

Everyone was scared of the motley band. No one protested their doings. The tramps even broke into a farmhouse and took food and goods.

"Do not tell a soul about us!" the Ruffler told the frightened farmer and his family. "Or we will come back and burn your house down!"

After a long walk, the group split up for

a while. Edward went with Hugo into a village.

"I see nothing to steal," Hugo remarked. "So we will beg instead."

Edward refused. How could *he* possibly beg? He was the king!

That angered Hugo. So he vowed to himself to make the boy suffer in the days to come.

Twice he stepped on Edward's toes the next day and pretended it was an accident. Then he did it a third time. But Edward had had enough. He hit Hugo with a thick stick as the tramps gathered to watch.

Hugo grabbed a stick, too, and the two began to fight. But Hugo was no match for the young boy. The finest teachers at the palace had trained Edward in swordsmanship.

After fifteen minutes of being battered, Hugo slunk away in disgrace. The rest of the tramps cheered.

Except for John Canty and Hugo, most of them had begun to like Edward. They admired his pluck and spirit. But he refused to help them steal and beg. And he was always trying to escape.

When they told him to rob a house, he

came out empty-handed. He had even warned the family inside!

Next, the Ruffler told Edward to help one of the outlaws, a tinker, with his work. Instead, Edward threatened the man with his own soldering iron. The tinker and Hugo had their hands full trying to keep Edward from running off.

In his dreams at night, Edward was king again. But each morning, he awoke in the outlaws' camp. Would this misery ever end?

One day, Hugo came up with a secret plan. He would take Edward out on a raid and get the boy arrested! Then he would be rid of the lad.

The two of them strolled to a nearby village. They drifted up and down the streets. Hugo was looking for the chance to steal something. And Edward was looking for a chance to escape.

Soon a woman approached. She carried a fat package in a basket. Hugo's eyes lit up.

When the woman had passed, he hissed to Edward, "Wait till I return!"

Hugo darted after her and snatched the package. The woman began to shout.

Hugo thrust the package into Edward's arms. "Race after me with the rest of them!

Cry, 'Stop, thief!' but lead them off my trail!" he told the boy.

The next minute, Hugo turned a corner and ran down an alley.

Edward was insulted! He threw the package on the ground, just as the woman arrived. A group of curious people was right behind her.

"How dare you!" the woman screamed. She grabbed Edward's wrist. The boy could not get free.

Hugo watched the action from behind a post. His enemy was caught, and the law would get him now. Hugo slipped away with a chuckle.

Edward kept struggling. "Let me go, you foolish creature!" he shouted to the woman. "I did not steal your goods!"

The crowd closed around the boy and called him names. A stout blacksmith threatened to teach Edward a lesson.

Suddenly a sword flashed through the air. It slapped against the blacksmith's arm.

"Let us proceed gently, not with unkind words and bad tempers," said the sword's owner pleasantly. "This is a matter for the law. Let go of the boy."

The blacksmith rubbed his arm and

moved away, muttering. The woman took her hand from Edward's wrist.

Edward sprang to his rescuer's side. It was Miles Hendon!

"You have come just in time, Sir Miles!" exclaimed Edward. "Now carve this crowd to bits!"

"Be quiet," Miles whispered to the king. "Trust me and all shall be well."

A policeman approached and placed his hand on the king's shoulder.

"Take your hand away," Miles said. "The boy will go peaceably. Lead on."

The officer led the woman with the package to court. Miles and Edward followed.

Edward did not want to go. But Miles said to him softly, "Think about it, Sire. As king, how can you ignore the law but require your subjects to obey?"

The king nodded. "You are right. If the king of England requires a subject to suffer under a law, the king must also suffer while he holds the position of a subject."

A judge listened to the case in court. The woman with the package swore that Edward was the thief.

The package was unwrapped. Inside was

a plump little pig. "What is this pig worth?" the judge asked.

The woman curtsied and replied, "Three shillings and eightpence."

The judge looked sad. "Maybe the lad was hungry," he said. "But if someone steals anything worth more than thirteen-pence, the law says he shall *hang* for it!"

Edward was startled, but he kept quiet. However, the woman grew pale.

"What have I done!" she cried, shaking with fright. "I do not want the poor boy hung! What shall I do?"

The judge said, "Give me a new value for the pig. I have not written down its worth yet."

"Call it eightpence, and be done with it!" the woman declared. She left the room with the pig under her arm. The police officer followed her.

Miles wondered why the officer had followed the woman. He slipped out and listened to the two speak in the hall.

"Sell me that pig for eightpence," the officer was saying.

"I will not," the woman replied. "I paid three shillings more for it myself!"

"You swore under oath to the judge it

was worth eightpence," the officer said. "Come back with me and answer for your lie! And the boy will hang."

"No, no," the woman said, trembling. "Here is the pig for eightpence." She handed it over and went off in tears.

Miles returned to the courtroom. After a speech to Edward, the judge sentenced him to a short term in jail.

Edward and Miles followed the officer toward the prison. "I will not enter a common jail!" Edward insisted to Miles.

"Trust me," Miles hissed to the king. "Just be patient."

When they came to an empty market square, Miles spoke to the officer. "Turn your back for a moment and let the poor lad escape," he said.

"What?" said the officer. "I will arrest you—"

"And I will tell the judge how you took the woman's pig for only eightpence!" Miles threatened. "You cheated her, and that is a crime—punishable by death!"

Cheaters were not punished by death. Miles was lying. But his threat worked. The fearful officer let Edward go, and soon he and Miles were on their way.

Chapter Ten
Hendon Hall

Half an hour later, the friends were jogging along a road on an old mule and an old donkey. Edward wore the secondhand suit that Miles had brought from the inn.

After traveling for a few days, the friends approached the Hendon family home. Miles had been looking forward to this. The road led through wide meadows. Cottages and orchards were scattered about.

They rode through the village, and Miles pointed out familiar sights: the church, the inn, the marketplace. At last, they reached Hendon Hall. They passed through a large stone gateway.

"Welcome to my home!" Miles exclaimed. He rushed into the mansion with Edward.

The first person Miles saw was his brother Hugh. He was writing a letter and stared haughtily at the intruder.

"Say you are glad to see me again,

Hugh!" cried Miles in excitement.

But Hugh said he did not recognize Miles.

"How can you not know me? I am your own brother!" Miles said.

Hugh shook his head sadly. "I wish it were so. But a letter came from overseas six or seven years ago. It said my brother died in battle."

"It was a lie!" Miles insisted. "Call our father; he will know who I am."

"I cannot. My father is dead."

"Dead?" Miles said. His voice trembled. "Let me see our brother Arthur. He will know me."

"He is also dead," Hugh replied.

"And the lady Edith? And the servants?" Miles asked.

Hugh assured him that Edith was living. He named the five servants that were still working at Hendon Hall. Then Hugh left the room to fetch Edith.

Miles was worried. Those five servants were dishonest. What had happened to the many good servants who had served the family faithfully?

Edward then spoke up gravely. "There are others in the world who also are not recognized, my good man. I do not doubt that you are Miles Hendon."

Miles felt guilty and confused. The boy believed in him. Yet Miles did not believe that this boy was truly the king.

Just then, the door opened. In walked the beautiful lady Edith. Her face was sad. She was followed by Hugh and some servants.

Miles ran over to Edith. "My darling Edith!" he cried.

Hugh waved him away. "Do you know this man?" Hugh asked Edith. She looked at Miles. The color drained from her face.

"I do not!" she said, then slowly turned and walked out of the room.

The servants also said they did not recognize Miles. Hugh turned to his brother.

"I fear there has been some mistake," he said with a slight sneer. "The servants do not know you. Neither does my wife—"

"Your *wife!*" exclaimed Miles. He grabbed Hugh around the throat and pinned him to the wall. "I see it all now!" he raged. "You wanted Edith and Hendon Hall all along. And now you've got them! It was you who wrote that letter saying I was dead!"

Miles pushed Hugh away in disgust. Hugh was enraged. He went to summon the police, leaving Miles and Edward alone.

"Hugh has always been a rascal," Miles muttered. Edward did not respond. He was busy thinking.

Then Edward looked up and said, "It is odd that the king of England is not missed. Why is no one searching for me? People should be distressed that the head of state has vanished. But I have not heard any proclamations about it. Could someone be playing the role of king in my place?"

"Poor ruined mind," Miles murmured to himself.

"But I have a plan that will help us," the king added. "I will write a letter in three languages—Latin, Greek, and English. You will take it to London in the morning and give it to my uncle Lord Hertford.

"When he sees it, he shall know I wrote it. Then he will send for me!"

Edward got to work and wrote the letter. Miles put in it his pocket just as Edith entered the room again.

"Please sit," Edith said to Miles. She sat

down herself and said, "Sir, I have come to warn you. I know you think you are our lost Miles. But do not stay here, for it is dangerous.

"My husband is master of this region, and powerful. He will tell everyone that you are an impostor."

She gazed intently at Miles. "Even if you *were* Miles Hendon—and Hugh believed it—he would still act the same. He is a tyrant who will destroy you.

"I myself have no freedom here. Miles and Arthur and their father are better off—they are free of him at last!

"You have attacked him in his own house. Now you must escape! If you have no money, take this purse. Bribe the servants to let you pass."

Miles refused the purse and stood up. He was certain that Edith really knew him. He figured that Hugh must have made her lie earlier.

"Tell me one thing," he said. "Look upon me. Am I Miles Hendon?"

"No," Edith said. Her eyes met his. "I do not know you."

"Swear it!"

"I swear," she said softly. "But you are wasting precious time. Save yourself!"

But it was too late. As she spoke, officers burst into the room. Soon Miles and Edward were bound and led to prison.

Chapter Eleven

In Prison

Wrapped in dirty blankets, Miles and Edward spent the night in jail. They could only hope that the day of Miles's trial would arrive soon.

Miles and Edward suffered for one long week. The noisy nights were filled with fights. During the daytime, people visited the prison and insulted Miles. He was known as the impostor.

But something new happened one day. The jailer brought in an old man. "Look around. See if you can pick out Miles Hendon," the jailer said to him.

Miles looked up and recognized the old man. He had been a loyal servant at Hendon Hall years before.

"This fellow was an honest man," Miles said to himself. "But he will lie like all the rest and say he does not know me."

Sure enough, the servant glanced around the room. "I see only scum of the streets here," he said to the jailer. "Which one is he?"

The jailer laughed and pointed to Miles. The old man approached Miles and looked carefully at him.

"This is no Hendon—and never was!" declared the old man.

"Your eyes are still good, old man!" said the jailer. "Give him a piece of your mind—everyone does. You'll find it fun."

The jailer walked out of the room. As soon as he had gone, the old man dropped to his knees.

"You have come back, my master!" he whispered to Miles. "I believed you were dead these past seven years. But you are alive! I knew it was you as soon as I saw you.

"I am old and poor, Sir Miles," the old servant added. "But say the word and I will go proclaim the truth...though I will be hanged for it!"

Miles refused to let him do that. But the old servant proved to be a worthy friend. Each day, he stopped by the jail and pretended to insult Miles. He always smuggled in food and news at the same time.

Bit by bit, the old servant told Miles

about the Hendon family during the past ten years. Miles's brother Arthur had died six years before. Edith had always hoped that Miles would return. But then the letter telling of Miles's death had arrived.

Miles's father fell ill from the sad news. Hugh and Edith were married at his deathbed.

But their marriage was not a happy one. It was said that the lady Edith had found a draft of the letter telling of Miles's death—and recognized the handwriting as her husband's! Had Hugh really written the letter himself? Nothing could be proven.

Edward listened to one piece of the servant's gossip with great interest.

"There is a rumor that the king is mad," the servant remarked.

Edward glared at the old man. "The king is *not* mad, my good man."

The servant was surprised at the boy's reaction. But he added, "The late king Henry the Eighth is to be buried in a day or two. And the new king will be crowned four days later."

"They must find him first," Edward muttered.

"Sir Hugh Hendon will attend the coronation," the servant went on. "He is in great favor with Lord Hertford, who is now the duke of Somerset."

"Since when is he a duke?" asked Edward sharply.

"Since the last day of January," the servant said. "The Great Council named him one, with the help of the king."

Edward was amazed. "*What* king?" he cried.

"Why, we have only one!" the servant replied, surprised again. "It is His Majesty King Edward the Sixth. A dear little urchin he is, too. He may be mad, but everyone hopes for a long reign. He has been kind and is destroying the cruelest laws of the land."

Edward was astounded. This "little urchin" sounded like the beggar boy he had left in the palace weeks ago, dressed in his own clothing.

It did not seem possible! How could that pauper boy have played a courtly role for so long? Tom's manners and speech were not princely. If he had pretended to be royal, he would have been thrown out of the palace. And the search for the real prince would have begun.

The more Edward tried to solve the mystery, the more confused he became. He slept poorly each night. And he could barely wait to get back to London.

Miles was not able to comfort the boy. But two kindly women in the prison became friends with Edward. He was grateful for their care, and he grew quite fond of them. They told him they were in prison because of their religion. "That is not a crime," Edward said. "You should not be jailed for it!"

The next morning, they were gone. "They have been freed!" Edward rejoiced. "But I will miss them greatly."

However, they had not been released. Instead, they had been taken and burned at the stake!

When Edward found this out, he was deeply shaken. What a terrible way to die! He knew he would never forget the horror of it.

The same day, several new prisoners were brought into the jail. Edward asked them why they were there. Their sad tales made his heart ache.

One woman had stolen a yard of cloth.

She was to be hanged for it!

A man was accused of killing a deer in the king's park. Now he was on the way to the gallows!

And a youth had found a hawk one day. It had escaped from its owner. The youth thought he could keep it and took it home. But the court ruled that he had stolen the hawk. So he was to be put to death!

Edward was furious. It was all so unfair and cruel! He vowed to change the laws once he was back in power as king. Then he would save these people's lives!

Chapter Twelve
To London

Miles's trial day finally arrived. He was found guilty of attacking the master of Hendon Hall. And he was sentenced to sit for two hours in the stocks.

Edward bitterly watched the crowd throw eggs at Miles in public. After this embarrassment, Miles was finally released. His sword was given back to him, along with his mule and donkey.

Sir Hugh Hendon had watched the spectacle with a wicked smile. He turned his horse around and galloped away, pleased with Miles's punishment.

As Miles rode off with Edward, he wondered what to do next. Where should he go to seek justice? How could he become the rightful master of Hendon Hall?

Then he remembered what his old servant had said about the young king and his goodness to others. Perhaps Miles could get the new king to listen to his story and help. But would the king be willing to even see a pauper such as Miles?

Their journey to London was smooth— until they reached the city itself. At ten o'clock on a cold February night, they stepped onto London Bridge.

It was the night before the new king was to be crowned. The bridge was filled with folks noisily celebrating and drinking. One man bumped into another. Suddenly a fight broke out.

Within ten minutes, the fight had become a wild riot. It stretched over several streets.

Miles and Edward were pulled in different directions by the noisy crowd. And they quickly lost track of each other in the confusion.

Chapter Thirteen

"I Do Not Know You, Woman!"

Edward Tudor was the true king of England. But for weeks, he had been wandering the countryside. He was poorly dressed and fed. He had spent time in jail with thieves and beggars.

During the same time, Tom Canty had been leading a very different life. At midnight on February 19, Tom went to bed feeling happy and excited. Tomorrow was Coronation Day, and he would be crowned king!

By now, Tom had become used to his royal role. He liked sitting on the throne and making decisions.

He liked hearing the trumpets and bugles at a state dinner. He liked hearing people call out, "Make way for the king!"

He was also used to his many servants and enjoyed the splendid clothes he wore each day.

He was kind and gentle to people who had been treated badly. He fought against unfair laws and changed them when he could.

But he was learning to be powerful in other ways, too. He could make earls and dukes tremble just by looking at them.

Did Tom ever think about the real prince who had switched clothes with him so many weeks before?

At first, Tom thought of Edward often. He longed for the prince to return.

But as time went on, Edward did not come back. And Tom was kept busy with many new things. So bit by bit, Tom forgot about the real prince.

He also stopped thinking about his own mother and sisters. At first, Tom missed them terribly. But after a while, he could not bear the idea of them coming to him in their rags. They would drag him back to the awful slums! And he did not want that to happen.

Once in a while, Tom did think about the real prince or his mother and sisters. But he felt ashamed and guilty when that happened. So he tried not to think of them at all.

Coronation Day began with a festive march

through the packed city streets.

Tom led the way on a prancing horse. Lord Hertford, now the duke of Somerset, followed with many nobles and guards. People cheered when Tom passed by.

"God save the king!" they cried.

Tom gazed joyfully at the crowds. Then in the distance, he spied two boys he knew from home. They were cheering, too.

Tom smiled to himself. The boys used to tease Tom when he pretended to be a prince in Offal Court. If only they knew that Tom was about to be crowned a real king!

But, of course, there was no way he could tell them who he was. It was too big a risk to take.

Tom flung handfuls of coins into the crowd. People scurried to pick up the money. The procession moved on, under arches and banners.

Suddenly a familiar woman's face appeared in the crowd. She pressed forward to see the young king.

It was Tom's own mother!

Tom was taken by surprise. His hand flew up in front of his eyes. And his palm faced outward toward the crowd.

In an instant, Tom's mother tore her way past the guards. She reached Tom's side and grabbed his leg, crying, "My child, my darling!"

A guard pulled the woman away. He pushed her back into the crush of people.

In a moment of panic, Tom exclaimed, "I do not know you, woman!"

The march continued toward Westminster Abbey. But Tom no longer enjoyed it. *I do not know you, woman!* The harsh words echoed in his head, and he felt ashamed. He had pretended not to know his own mother!

The duke of Somerset noticed the change in Tom as they rode along. The boy did not look happy anymore.

The crowds lining the roads noticed the change in Tom, too. They stopped cheering as loudly as before. Their faces looked anxious.

The duke rode up alongside Tom. "My lord," he whispered to him, "the people see that you are sad. They take it as an omen—a sign of something bad to come!

"That beggar woman has bothered you, I can tell. But you must stop dreaming and lift up your head."

Tom turned to look at the duke. "She was my mother!" he said sadly.

The duke shuddered. Had the king gone mad again?

Chapter Fourteen
The Crowning of the King

Royal ladies, foreign ambassadors, and the king's procession filled Westminster Abbey.

Tom entered the cathedral wearing a long robe of gold cloth. He stepped onto a platform, and the entire crowd rose. The solemn coronation ceremony began.

As the audience watched, Tom's face grew paler and paler, and he trembled.

How could switching clothes with Edward Tudor so many weeks ago end like this? Tom could barely listen to the ceremony.

At last, the final act of coronation arrived. The archbishop of Canterbury lifted up the crown from its cushion. He held the crown over the mock king's head. The vast room was hushed.

Suddenly a ragged and dirty barefoot boy appeared, striding up the cathedral's aisle. No one, not even the guards at the door, had noticed him until that moment. The boy stopped and raised his hand.

"I forbid you to set the crown of England upon that head!" he warned. "*I* am the king!"

Instantly several people grabbed the bareheaded boy. But Tom stepped forward in his regal robes and proclaimed, "Let him go! He *is* the king!"

The entire crowd was bewildered. Who was this strange boy?

The duke of Somerset was confused, too. But he quickly called out, "Do not mind His Majesty! His madness is on him again. Seize the vagabond!"

Tom stamped his foot. "Do not touch him! He is the king!"

No one moved. The ragged boy stepped onto the platform, and Tom fell on his knees in front of him.

"Oh, my lord the king, let poor Tom Canty swear his loyalty to you!" Tom cried.

The duke of Somerset and the other nobles watched this odd scene in silence. They noticed something surprising. There was a striking resemblance between the two boys. Their faces and builds looked identical!

"I wish to ask certain questions—" began the duke.

"I will answer them, my lord," replied the newcomer.

The duke asked him questions about the dead king, the court, the princesses, and even the prince himself. The boy answered all of them correctly. He was even able to describe the private rooms in the palace.

Everyone agreed that it was strange and wonderful. The duke of Somerset shook his head.

"It is wonderful indeed, but our king can do the same," he pointed out. "It does not mean that this boy is the king."

Tom was worried. He was losing all hope. Soon he would be stuck upon the throne and never be with his mother again. And this boy, the true king, would be pushed back into the streets!

The duke was busy thinking. Then he turned to the ragged boy and posed a new question.

"Where is the Great Seal of England, which vanished a while ago? Only the boy who has been the true Prince of Wales will know that!"

Everyone nodded happily. There was no way this impostor could know the answer!

To the lords' surprise, the boy spoke up at once to one of the lords. "My lord St. John, go to my private rooms in the palace. Look in the left corner farthest from the bedroom door.

"Near the floor there is a nail in the wall," the boy continued. "Press it and a little jeweled closet will open. No one knows about this but me—and the man who built it!

"The first thing that you see there will be the Great Seal. Fetch it here!"

Everyone wondered how this strange boy knew St. John's name.

Tom turned to the lord and said sharply, "You have heard the king's command. Now go!"

Soon St. John returned to the cathedral. As he came up the aisle, all talking stopped.

"Sire, the Great Seal is not there!" he said to Tom.

The duke of Somerset called out angrily, "Cast the beggar into the street!"

Guards sprang to obey, but Tom Canty waved them away. "Whoever touches the boy risks his own life!" he declared.

The duke of Somerset thought for a

moment. He was perplexed. "How could a bulky item like the Great Seal of England just vanish?" he asked Lord St. John. "It is so large and golden—"

"Is it round?" Tom cried excitedly. "With letters engraved on it? Oh, I know what this Great Seal is! You could have had it three weeks ago if you had only described it to me! I do know where it is."

He pointed to the ragged boy and added, "But the rightful king of England put it there first! And he himself shall tell you where it is. Then you will believe that he knew its location on his own."

Tom begged the poor boy to try and remember where the Great Seal was. "It was the last thing you did weeks ago!" he reminded the lad. "It was right before you rushed out of the palace, dressed in my rags, to punish the soldier that hurt me."

Everyone looked at the newcomer. He stood thinking with his head bowed. His future depended on recalling this one little fact!

But at last, the boy sighed and shook his head. "I remember the scene with you," he said tremblingly to Tom. "But nothing at all about the Great Seal."

Chapter Fifteen
The Great Seal

"Wait! Do not give up!" Tom cried in a panic. To help the boy, he checked off the details of their first meeting.

"We talked about my sisters, Nan and Bet," Tom said. "And about the games in Offal Court. Ah, good, you remember that!

"Then for a jest, we exchanged clothes. We stood before a mirror. And we looked exactly alike!"

"I do recall that, too," the boy said with a nod.

"You saw that my hand was hurt," Tom continued. "You wanted to punish the soldier who had hurt me, and you ran to the door.

"On the way, you passed a table with the Great Seal lying on it. You snatched it up and looked around for a hiding place—"

"Yes, yes! You have said enough!" the dirty boy exclaimed happily. "St. John, fetch the Seal! You will find it in the suit of armor hanging on the wall of my bedroom."

St. John departed at once. The nobles filling the cathedral talked excitedly among themselves. Minutes ticked by as the crowd waited for the lord to return.

At last, St. John re-entered Westminster Abbey and mounted the platform. He raised his hand high. He was holding the Great Seal!

A shout went up: "Long live the true king!"

For five minutes, the air was filled with happy shouts and the clash of musical instruments. People wildly waved white handkerchiefs.

The real king proudly stood on the platform as the nobles bowed down to him.

"Now, my king, take these regal garments back," Tom pleaded. "And give me—your poor servant—my rags again."

"Let the impostor be thrown into the Tower of London!" ordered the duke of Somerset.

But the new king objected. "Let no one harm the boy! If it hadn't been for Tom Canty, I would not have my crown back," he pointed out.

The king then kindly asked Tom, "How were you able to remember where I hid the Seal when I myself could not?"

"Ah, that was easy," Tom said. "I used it many times."

"But you did not know what it was," the king said. "So how did you use it? Speak up, good lad! You have nothing to fear."

Tom blushed. He was embarrassed. "I used the Seal to crack nuts!" he stammered finally.

The crowd laughed heartily on hearing this confession.

Then the royal robe was passed from Tom Canty to Edward Tudor—and the real king was crowned!

Chapter Sixteen

Edward as King

And what had happened to Miles Hendon after the riot on London Bridge?

Hour after hour, for a day and a half, Miles searched for Edward. He tramped through streets and alleys. But Edward was nowhere to be found.

Miles finally reached Westminster Palace the day after Coronation Day. He was tired and hungry. He sat down to rest on a bench right outside the palace.

Some officers were passing by. They saw the ragged man sitting on a bench and promptly arrested him. Miles tried to explain who he was, but they did not listen. Instead, the officers searched him for any weapons. But all they found was a letter.

One officer tore it open. Miles smiled when he saw the letter. It was the one that Edward had written weeks before in Hendon Hall. The letter was in English, Greek, and Latin.

The officer scowled when he read the

English part. "Here's another rascal who claims the crown!" the officer exclaimed. "Hold him, men, while I go tell the king."

By and by, the officer returned. This time, he was very polite. He bowed and asked Miles to follow him.

The guards escorted Miles into the palace, through long halls, and up a grand staircase. They entered the throne room. It was filled with people.

The king was sitting on his throne, conducting business. But he looked just like Edward! Miles could not believe his eyes.

"Is it a dream?" Miles wondered to himself. "Or was my young friend telling the truth? Could he really be the king and not a pauper, after all?"

An idea quickly came to him. He walked over to a chair, picked it up, and set it in front of the king. Then he boldly sat down on it.

A guard roughly grabbed him. "Get up! You may not sit in the presence of the king!"

But the king stretched out his hand. "Do not touch him!" he cried. "It is his right!"

The crowd looked amazed. Just then,

Sir Hugh Hendon and the lady Edith entered the room. They looked confused at the goings-on, and gazed in shock from the king to the ragged Miles and back to the king again.

"This is my trusted and beloved servant Miles Hendon," the king went on. "He saved my life when I was a prince! For that, he was made a knight. I will also name him an earl for all that he has done to help me.

"And he has been granted the right to sit in the presence of royalty, now and forever."

The king looked around the room and then spied Hugh.

"Take the stolen land away from this robber!" he proclaimed. "And lock him up until I have need of him."

Sir Hugh was led away.

There was a stir at the far end of the vast room. Tom, now clothed in new garments, approached the throne and knelt down.

"I have heard of the good things that you have done these past few weeks," Edward said gently to Tom. "You have ruled with mercy and kindness."

The king promised to help Tom's

mother and sisters. They would never be poor again.

He also ordered that Tom's rich new garments be worn only by Tom. That way, everyone would know that Tom was protected by the king.

Tom rose and bowed to the king. Then he ran off to tell the good news to his mother, Nan, and Bet.

Miles would not press charges against Sir Hugh. So Hugh was never punished for his bad deeds. But he finally left his wife and went to live far away in shame.

Miles Hendon, now the earl of Kent, married Lady Edith.

John Canty, Tom's father, was never heard of again.

Edward VI, king of England, had not forgotten the people he had met in prison. He rescued those that he could.

And for the rest of their lives, the king and Tom were fond of telling the amazing tale of the prince and the pauper!

MARK TWAIN was born in Missouri in 1835. He was a journalist and lecturer and wrote several great stories and novels. Among his most famous books are *The Adventures of Huckleberry Finn, A Connecticut Yankee in King Arthur's Court,* and *The Prince and the Pauper,* which was published in 1881.

Twain died in 1910 in Hartford, Connecticut, when he was seventy-five years old.

JANE E. GERVER is a children's book author and editor, who grew up with identical twin brothers. Her dozens of books written for children range from pre-school board books to middle-grade fiction. She lives in New York City with her husband.